Nina
Fairy Ballerina

New Girl

Anna Wilson

Illustrated by Nicola Slater

MACMILLAN CHILDREN'S BOOKS

First published 2006 by Macmillan Children's Books
a division of Macmillan Publishers Limited
20 New Wharf Road, London N1 9RR
Basingstoke and Oxford
www.panmacmillan.com

Associated companies throughout the world

ISBN-13: 978-0-330-43985-5
ISBN-10: 0-330-43985-5

3 5 7 9 8 6 4

A CIP catalogue record for this book is available from
the British Library.

Typeset by Nigel Hazle
Printed and bound in Great Britain by Mackays of Chatham plc, Kent

Anna Wilson lives in a village in

For Mum and Dad with love

Chapter One

Down in the roots of the horse-chestnut tree, Nina stared glumly out of her little round bedroom window and sighed. The huge brown leaves drifted slowly down and Nina's fairy friends shrieked with delight as they waved their wands, turning the leaves into boats and carriages.

They called out to Nina, trying to get her to join in the fun.

"Come on, Nina! Stop sulking and come outside!"

"What's the matter with her today?" asked Nina's friend Blossom, who'd just turned a large leaf into a parachute, and was amusing herself launching off a nearby branch and crashing into her friends below.

"Don't pay any attention to old grumpy there," called Poppy, Nina's little sister. "*The Letter* still hasn't arrived, has it?"

"Ah." Blossom smiled weakly. "I forgot. Poor Nina."

Every morning Nina had been setting her dandelion clock for half past six so that she could be up in time to catch the post. This morning was no different. While her friends were outside having fun, Nina was waiting for the letter that would change her life. The letter that would make all her dreams come true. The letter . . .

"Hey, Neeny-Meany!" Poppy yelled, jolting Nina out of her thoughts. Poppy was hovering annoyingly in front of the window, flicking conker shells at her.

"Ouch! That's sharp! Just stop it, will you, and leave me alone, Soppy," Nina snapped.

"OK then, I'll go. I suppose you won't want to see the letter that's just arrived by grasshopper express then," Poppy smirked, and made as if to fly off.

"Wait! Grasshopper? Express? It must be something really important.

Oh! Could it be . . . ?" Nina flew straight out of the window and chased after her sister. "Let me see it, Soppy. Give it here!"

"You'll have to be nice to me!" Poppy sang out, waving something shiny at her sister as she flitted around a branch.

"That's enough, Poppy," came a stern voice.

"Mum! I was just going to—" Poppy stammered.

"Give the letter to Nina – now!" their mother commanded.

The three fairies drifted down to the ground. This was the moment Nina had been waiting for. She sat down on a mushroom and stared at the shimmering envelope in front of her. She gazed at the beautiful gold, wispy writing that threaded itself over the front of the envelope and whispered to herself:

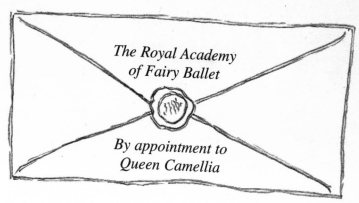

Nina Dewdrop
4 The Chestnuts
Little Frolic-by-the-Stream

Then she turned the envelope over and gasped at the royal crest on the back.

*The Royal Academy
of Fairy Ballet*

*By appointment to
Queen Camellia*

She started to pull the paper apart, gingerly, and then couldn't wait a moment longer and gave it a rip. A shower of silver sparks filled the air and tinkling music floated out, followed by

the tiniest fairy Nina had ever seen.
Immediately the fairy opened a scroll she
was carrying and began to sing:

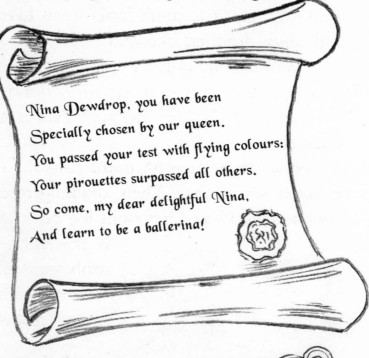

Nina Dewdrop, you have been
Specially chosen by our queen.
You passed your test with flying colours:
Your pirouettes surpassed all others.
So come, my dear delightful Nina,
And learn to be a ballerina!

With that the fairy rolled
the scroll up in silver
ribbon, handed it to Nina
and promptly disappeared.
Nina couldn't speak. She
stared at the scroll in her hand,

her eyes wide and her mouth hanging open.

"Well, say something, dopey," Poppy said nastily. "You don't look much like a ballerina, drooling like that."

"Will you be quiet, Poppy!" Mrs Dewdrop snapped, and turned to Nina, beaming. "Well done, darling! This is so exciting."

Nina jumped up on tiptoe and hugged her mother. Then, giggling and smiling, she kicked her right leg back in a graceful arabesque and swished off to show

Blossom the scroll.

"We knew she could do it, didn't we,

Poppy?" Mrs Dewdrop clasped her hands together and sighed.

Poppy snarled. All summer it had been "Nina this, ballerina that." It was enough to drive a fairy frantic. Poppy thought back bitterly to how this nonsense had all started.

In the spring the school in Little Frolic-by-the-Stream had a special visitor. Magnolia Valentine, the most famous prima ballerina in fairyland, had come to give a talk. She had told spellbinding stories about her dancing career: tales of glamour and glitz, of dancing for princes and princesses from other lands.

What had captured the fairies' imagination more than anything were Magnolia's stories of her time at the Royal Academy of Fairy Ballet.

"I made friends for life at the Academy," Magnolia murmured, gazing dreamily around the school hall. "When

you live and dance together like that,
special bonds are formed that last
forever."

Nina already loved her ballet lessons
with her teacher, Miss Thistle. After
meeting Magnolia Valentine she had
talked of nothing else for days.

Poppy had not been so easily
impressed. "Magnolia Valentine?
Magnolia Past-her-prime, more like. If
ballet's so blooming brilliant, Nina, why
don't you fly off to the Academy right
away and leave us in peace?" she had
grumbled.

She had lived to regret that suggestion
when Nina applied to take that year's
entrance exam for the Academy's annual
scholarship award. There was only one
scholarship granted each year, and Nina
practised hard all term for the exam.

"And now she's gone and won it!"
muttered Poppy, fuming. Her wings were

fluttering with indignation; she could
hardly keep her feet on the ground.
"We'll never hear the last of it now!"

Chapter Two

Written on the scroll that the tiny fairy had given Nina was "A Complete and Comprehensive List of Equipment Needed at the Academy". And that could only mean one thing.

"Shopping!" squealed Nina excitedly. "Can we go now, Mum? Can we? Please!"

"All right, all right. Calm down, Nina, you're getting your wings in a twist. Go and put your shoes on and then we can go."

Poppy was still sulking.

"Oh, do stop fuming like that, Poppy dear. It's not very fairylike!" Mrs Dewdrop laughed. "I'm sure we can find something for you at the shops too."

Poppy perked up a bit and started quietly planning what to buy.

"I must have that toy unicorn from Spellsbury's. The one that grants three wishes and then turns into the pet of your choice. And *everyone* in my class had new petal skirts for PE last year, so I want a new one too. And—"

Poppy's daydreaming was interrupted by a loud crash.

"POPPY! What have you done now?" shouted her mother, surveying the devastation. Poppy had been hovering around the room making her mental shopping list, and she hadn't looked where she was going. She had caught her wand on the edge of the kitchen dresser and set the acorn cups and saucers flying in all directions.

"You just can't stay out of trouble, can you? You're so clumsy! There's no chance of *you* becoming a ballerina, that's for sure." Mrs Dewdrop sighed. "Come on, let's get going, girls."

Little Frolic didn't have very many shops, so the Dewdrops had to catch a dragonfly to the nearest fairy city, Hornbeamster.

"Why can't we fly on our own, Mum?" Poppy asked. Poppy liked whizzing along at her own pace and hated having to sit still.

"You know why, darling. It's too congested," her mother explained

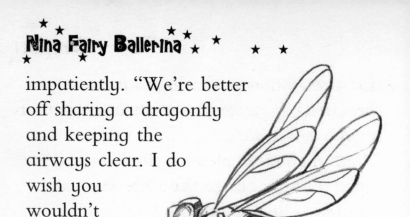

impatiently. "We're better off sharing a dragonfly and keeping the airways clear. I do wish you wouldn't always ask me the same thing."

Nina liked going by dragonfly. It was speedy and silent and she could spend time dreaming about ballet instead of looking where she was going. Flying on your own could be exhausting, as you had to look out for careless fairies who overtook with no warning.

The dragonfly the Dewdrops had caught today was a particularly nippy model, and very sleek, with shimmering emerald bodywork and an impressive set of silver wings. She swooped low to avoid the traffic jams in the high lanes and brought her passengers to their destination ahead of schedule.

"All change, please," she hummed quietly. "All change. You are now at Hornbeamster Central."

"We can see that," Poppy muttered, giving the dragonfly a sullen stare.

But Nina and her mother were too excited to pay any attention to Poppy's mood this time.

"Oh, it's ages since we've been to Hornbeamster!" trilled Mrs Dewdrop. "Look, there's the big dandelion clock in the main square. Now, it's eleven o'clock. If we get separated, make sure you meet back there, under the clock, at two. All right, girls?"

First on Nina's list was, of course, ballet shoes.

"We'll have to go to Bushel and Broomley for them, Mum, won't we?"

Nina said excitedly. "They always have the biggest selection."

"Yes, here we are. In you go then, Poppy. Follow Nina and don't dawdle."

Nina felt overwhelmed whenever she went to Bushel & Broomley. No sooner did she find one pair of shoes that she simply had to have than another pair would float off the shelves and hang in front of her as if to say, "What about us?"

This time, however, Nina was focused – it was ballet shoes only that she was interested in. So surely that would be simple enough.

WHOOSH!
Suddenly Nina was surrounded by a cloud of ballet shoes of every style, size and colour imaginable.

"Enough!" cried Mrs Dewdrop, and the shoes scurried back to the shelves, hanging their ribbons mournfully. Fairy ballet shoes don't like being told off.

"Who could have made them do that, I wonder?" said Mrs Dewdrop, looking around thoughtfully.

A sneaky-looking Poppy slunk off behind a shelf of trainers, waving her wand surreptitiously.

"OUCH!" cried Nina, staring down at her feet. A pair of very small black ballet shoes had attached themselves to her and were crushing her toes.

"I didn't ask for these shoes!" Nina gasped. "They're killing my feet! Get them off!"

"Do try and use a bit of common-magic now and again, dear," her mother sighed. "Just ask them to go away – politely."

"Please – go – back – to the – shelves!" Nina hissed between gritted teeth.

The black ballet shoes immediately left her and went to join the other pairs on the shelves.

"Ah! That's better," Nina sighed, rubbing her sore toes. "Now, let's look at the list. It says I should have two pairs of everyday ballet shoes in regulation turquoise, and one special pair for performing. Oh, there are so many to choose from! What about those pretty silver ones with the daisies?" Nina waved her wand at a dainty pair of silk ballet shoes with ribbons made from daisy chains. The shoes floated towards her and landed softly at her feet.

"You must be practical, Nina," Mrs Dewdrop said gently. "Daisy-chain ribbons are so difficult to look after."

"But, Mum, these would be perfect as performance shoes, wouldn't they?" Nina pleaded. She was so busy trying to persuade her mother to buy the daisy shoes that she didn't notice what Poppy was up to.

"Ribbit!"

"Urgh!" Nina squealed, jumping back in surprise. "Who put those frogs there? And where have the daisy shoes gone?"

There was a snigger from behind the shelving.

"Come out this instant, Poppy Dewdrop," her mother scolded, "and give me your wand. If you can't use it wisely, you won't use it at all. Changing shoes into frogs – I ask you! I've had enough of your mischief. Go and wait on that bench outside the shop until Nina and I have finished."

Poppy left the shop, muttering and sulking.

"I'll just have to entertain myself, won't I?" she said under her breath. "Who cares about sissy old ballet anyway?" She choked back a sob and sat down to think.

Back inside Bushel & Broomley, Nina had still not managed to persuade her mother to buy the daisy shoes. She had settled instead for a pair of pink-and-violet ballet shoes with easy-to-tie bulrush ribbons. With a final longing glance at the daisy shoes, Nina went to join her mother at the till.

"Please send the shoes to our home address by hummingbird-mail," Mrs Dewdrop instructed the shop assistant, writing her details on the lily pad by the till. Then Nina and her mother went outside to join Poppy.

But she was nowhere to be seen.

Chapter Three

"Where can she have gone?" Mrs Dewdrop gasped, spinning round to scan the streets for Poppy.

Nina tried to calm her down. "She can't have gone far, Mum. She probably got bored and went for a walk. You told her to meet us under the big dandelion clock if we got separated, didn't you? She'll be all right."

"But she's still so little!" Mrs Dewdrop wailed. "And she's probably upset about you going to the Academy – I should have thought of that. I must go and find her. Listen, you know where Arabesque's is, don't you, Nina?" Nina nodded. "Well, you go there and start trying on tutus. I'll find Poppy. Just DON'T leave the shop until I come back."

Before Nina could say another word, her mother had disappeared in a flurry of rosy sparkles.

Nina wasn't worried about her sister. Poppy was forever getting into trouble, but she always seemed to find her own way out again. At this moment in time, tutus were the most pressing item on Nina's agenda.

She looked at her Comprehensive List from the Academy and fluttered off to Arabesque's.

After Bushel & Broomley, Arabesque's was Nina's favourite shop in the whole of fairyland. The sign outside boasted:

We cater for all your needs

Below this was
a revolving
door that
piped out some
music from
Swan Lake as it
spun Nina out
into the shop.

Nina flew
over to the
shop's floor
plan and
started looking
for where she
could find
tutus and
leotards. She
was so
engrossed in
the list of different departments that she
didn't notice someone come up behind
her.

"Is that a list from the Royal Academy you've got there, dear?" said a sing-song voice.

Nina jumped and looked up – and up – at the speaker.

The fairy who'd spoken was at least twice the size of Nina and he was perpetually patting his long blond hair and fussing with his glittery uniform.

"I'm Flax," said the overgrown fairy, "and judging from what I can see on that scroll, *you* must be heading for the Academy! Don't worry," Flax continued, smiling down at Nina, "I know everything there is to know about ballet, beautiful! That's why I look after all you little prima ballerinas. Now, enough about me; show me The List." Flax bowed dramatically, sweeping his right arm forward in a flourish.

Nina shook her head in astonishment and handed over her tiny scroll.

Flax read it through. "Let's see. Yes,

Nina Fairy Ballerina

yes, it all seems to be here:

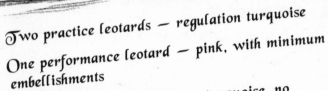

Two practice leotards — regulation turquoise

One performance leotard — pink, with minimum embellishments

Two crossover cardigans — turquoise, no embroidery

Two practice tutus — turquoise, no frills

One performance tutu — choose from Academy-approved selection

Seven pairs leg warmers — silk, turquoise, standard issue

Seven pairs pink tights — good fit, no wrinkles

One snack box — pink, with silver clasps

One suitcase — hard-wearing silver birch

One ballet bag — turquoise, with Academy crest

Nina was mesmerized by the selection of shimmering tutus that Flax brought her to try on. She was so busy curtseying at her reflection in the shop's many mirrors that she jumped a mile when she heard her mother's voice: "Nina! Haven't you finished yet?"

Mrs Dewdrop was furious. She had found Poppy cavorting in the town fountain. The youngest Dewdrop fairy was now dripping wet and trailing weed and sludge.

"Soppy Poppy!" Nina laughed.

"That's enough, Nina. Poppy, go and clean yourself up," snapped Mrs Dewdrop.

While a scowling Poppy scuttled off to the loo to get dry, Nina

made her final choice of tutu: an Academy-approved violet one with tiny gold daisies stitched all over it. When I eventually get my hands on those daisy shoes, this tutu will match perfectly, she thought to herself.

Chapter Four

The shopping trip to Hornbeamster had made Nina more excited than ever about going to the Academy. She spent the next few days doing nothing but preparing for her new school. She immersed herself in ballet books, reading stories about her favourite ballerinas. Every morning she practised the routines that she'd learned at ballet class.

Meanwhile, Poppy had given up on her mischievous magic for now and was constantly interrupting Nina to ask her about ballet.

"Come on, Nina," she pleaded, "show
me that pirouette again – if you're going
to bore my wings off I may as well learn
something."

Nina pirouetted perfectly, ending in a
neat fifth position. Poppy tried to copy
her and fell in a crumpled heap on the
floor with one
foot stuck
underneath her.

"Humpf!
Well, it looks a
lot easier when
you do it,"
Poppy said
sulkily, raking
her hands
through her
chestnut curls
and shaking out
her wings.

"Miss Thistle
always told us

'practice makes perfect'," said Nina
primly.

"S'pose so," Poppy grumbled. "Come
on then, let's practise."

Nina willingly took on the role of
teacher. She wanted to show Poppy all
five ballet positions.

"First position is easy, Poppy. You just
stand straight, hold your hands down
gracefully in front of you . . . that's it!
Now, keep your heels together, and open
out your toes."

"What do you mean, 'open out your
toes'?" Poppy said. "I'm not a monkey."

Nina sighed and grasped Poppy's feet,
pulling them into the correct position.

"It's no good, Nina," Poppy whined.
"My feet are like bananas compared to
yours."

Nina giggled. "Tell you what, let's do
something easier. Sit down a minute," she
suggested. "I'll show you an exercise to
help you point your toes." Poppy pulled

a face. "It'll be fun – promise!" Nina assured her.

Nina ran over to her dressing table and turned on her Daisy Discplayer. Bars of bouncy music from *The Nutcracker* came wafting out.

"This is the bit where the toy soldier dances," she explained.

Poppy just raised her eyebrows and muttered, "So what?" Nevertheless, she watched carefully as Nina showed her how to play "Good Toes, Naughty Toes".

When Nina called out, "Good toes,"
the fairies both had to point their toes
down as far as they would go. Then she
shouted, "Naughty toes," and they had
to stick their feet up straight and wag
their finger at them, as if they were
telling them off. The music got faster
and faster, and Nina called out her
commands quicker and quicker in time to

the music. Soon the sisters were rolling around in a hysterical heap on the floor, as they couldn't keep up.

Maybe being a ballerina isn't such a bore after all, Poppy thought to herself. But she wouldn't admit this to Nina.

At last the time had come to leave Little Frolic. The Dewdrops were soon on their way by dragonfly to the Royal Academy of Fairy Ballet in Oakton. Nina was feeling nervous and excited at the same time. It had been sad saying goodbye to her friends, especially Blossom, and now Nina couldn't stop worrying about being the new girl. To take her mind off things she chatted away non-stop to her mother and Poppy.

All too soon, the three fairies arrived. Nina gasped as she looked up at the glittering gold gates surrounding the roots of the oak tree which housed the Academy. A bell hung from a silk rope

and next to it was a sign that shimmered with the words:

> *Welcome to the*
> *Royal Academy of Fairy Ballet.*
>
> *Please ring for assistance.*

Suddenly a tiny fairy appeared, just like the one who'd brought Nina's acceptance letter. She curtseyed to Nina and sang out:

> *Come in, Nina – don't delay!*
> *Now's your lucky chance*
> *For here at the Academy*
> *You'll learn to leap and dance!*

Nina beamed at the little fairy, then reached up and tugged on the silk rope. A cluster of golden bells tinkled out the first few bars of *Coppélia*, and immediately

a member of the Academy staff fluttered
into view. This fairy was wearing a
crossover cardigan and a shiny tutu with
a fluffy skirt, all in the Academy's
regulation turquoise. She had a badge
that said "Peach Meadowsweet –
Academy Secretary".

"Good morning," trilled the fairy as
she unlocked the gates. "I'm Miss
Meadowsweet. I work in the office. And
you are . . . ?" she enquired politely.

"Nina Dewdrop, miss," Nina
muttered nervously.

"Ah! The scholarship girl!" Miss
Meadowsweet smiled kindly. "I've heard
a lot about you. Quite a talent, I'm told!
And this must be your sister. What's your
name, little one?"

"Poppy," Poppy said rather
aggressively. She didn't much like being
called "little one".

Miss Meadowsweet raised her
eyebrows and turned to Mrs Dewdrop.

"Have you got accommodation in town, Mrs Dewdrop?" she asked.

Mrs Dewdrop explained that she and Poppy were staying in Oakton for a couple of days to help Nina settle in at the Academy. Miss Meadowsweet suggested that Nina's mother go and check in now while Nina went to the Grand Hall with the other pupils.

"Come, Nina. Everyone's meeting there for registration."

"What about me?" asked Poppy stroppily.

"You can watch if you like," Miss Meadowsweet said reluctantly. "But you'll have to wait outside the hall."

"Yes, and make sure you behave yourself, Pops," Nina said quietly.

Poppy stuck her tongue out at her sister and then smiled sweetly at her mother. "Please, Mum? Can I stay?" she asked.

Mrs Dewdrop agreed and bent to kiss both her girls.

"Be good fairies now," she said. "And have fun. I'll come and meet you for lunch."

Nina could hardly believe her eyes as Miss Meadowsweet whisked her and Poppy through the entrance hall of the Academy. The walls were covered in portraits of beautiful, famous ballerinas: Clematis Thistledown, Celandine Rosebud – and of course Nina's heroine, Magnolia Valentine.

If only I could learn to dance as
gracefully as these ballerinas! Nina
thought to herself.

When they got to the Grand Hall,
Miss Meadowsweet motioned to Poppy to
sit on a bench outside, then she ushered
Nina in. The Grand Hall certainly lived
up to its name. On the ceiling there were
four vast chandeliers hanging from huge

soft-pink rosebuds. Each chandelier was lit up by hundreds and hundreds of tiny fireflies. The oak-panelled walls were decorated with garlands of blossom and berries and there were sparkling mirrors everywhere.

At the front of the hall was a stage with a row of golden throne-like chairs. Each chair was occupied by a stern-looking fairy. They must be the teachers, thought Nina nervously. They don't look as friendly as the ones at my *old* school.

Each fairy teacher had her hair drawn up into a very tight bun and they were all sitting upright, their heads held high and their tutus crisply starched. Not one of them was smiling.

The Grand Hall was filled with row upon row of budding fairy ballerinas, standing as tall as they could: tummies in, bottoms in, all in perfect first position and not a naughty toe in sight. Nina felt very scruffy and small as Miss Meadowsweet led her to the front and addressed the sternest-looking teacher of them all:

"Good morning, Madame Dupré. This is Nina Dewdrop."

"Madame Dupré!" gasped Nina. Madame Dupré was the headmistress of the Academy and had been one of the judges at Nina's audition.

"Nina, of course! The scholarship fairy. I remember your pliés showed great promise."

Madame Dupré stood up and her fearsome features relaxed into a gentle, welcoming smile. "Welcome to the Royal Academy."

Nina turned and looked at Miss Meadowsweet, feeling absolutely petrified.

"Curtsey, Nina! Curtsey!" Miss Meadowsweet whispered.

Nina curtseyed rather clumsily and teetered, nearly losing her balance. A group of fairies began to giggle.

"That's enough!" Madame Dupré barked at the sniggering fairies. Nina blushed furiously as a tall, blonde fairy stuck her tongue out at her. Miss Meadowsweet patted Nina on the shoulder. "You'll be fine, Nina," she assured her. "Go and stand with the other First Years now." Nina did as she was told.

Madame Dupré cleared her throat. "Now that we are all here, let us begin. Good morning, Academy!"

Nina jumped in surprise as the whole Academy responded in unison by curtseying and calling out, "Good morning, Madame Dupré!" She decided to watch everyone else very carefully so that she would know exactly what to do.

During assembly, Madame Dupré read out several notices, most of which were for the benefit of the new fairies. Nina began to feel more relaxed as she found out which class she would be in. She was also given a map of the Academy and a list of the rules. She discovered that all the new fairies were sharing rooms with each other.

"All the new girls will have a mentor too," Madame explained. "A fairy from the year above will be assigned to each pair of room-mates to show you around and help you to settle in. Your mentors will stay with you all day today to make sure you do not get lost. And now, it simply remains for me to welcome you all to a new year at the Royal Academy." She smiled at the ranks of fairy ballerinas looking up at her. "I have a feeling this is going to be a very exciting year indeed."

Chapter Five

Nina hurried out of the hall to find Poppy looking very fed up.

"That was so boring," Poppy complained. "I couldn't hear a thing."

"Cheer up, Soppy! At least now you'll get to see my room and meet my room-mate," Nina said, trying to sound brave. "Come on, I'm on Charlock corridor. You can help me read the map."

Nina took her sister by the hand and the fairies flew off, dodging the crowds of budding ballerinas flocking out of the Grand Hall.

"Here we are – Charlock," Nina said
finally, reading the sign on a pink door
with ballet shoes painted all over it. She
turned the handle and went into the
corridor to find her room. "I'm in room
five apparently," Nina added. "Ah, here
we are."

The room was very cosy. There was
a large round window looking out across
a field of wild flowers. The window sill
was deep and was piled high with comfy
rainbow-striped velvet cushions.

There were two little beds covered
with soft patchwork quilts and scattered
with big fluffy pillows. The walls were

painted a light shade of pink and the
ceiling was blue with white fluffy clouds.
Someone had already started putting
some posters up: pictures of ballet shoes
and famous fairy ballerinas, and posters
from ballet shows.

Nina spotted her luggage in a pile by
the window. She was just about to ask
Poppy to help her unpack when a fairy
darted into the room
and flew on to one of
the beds, landing in a
giggling heap.

"Hi! Isn't this
great? I'm so
excited I could
turn into a
firework!" the
fairy cried,
bouncing
up and
down on
her bed.

She was very pretty, Nina noticed. She had bright orangey-red spiky hair and green eyes that glittered like emeralds.

"You look like a firework already," Poppy muttered.

"Hello," Nina said timidly. "I'm Nina Dewdrop. Are you my room-mate?"

"Looks like it!" the fairy replied. "I'm Periwinkle Moonshine – but you can call me Peri. Who's this?" Peri went on breathlessly, pointing at Poppy.

"*This*," Poppy said, "is Poppy. And you can call me Poppy."

"She's my little sister," Nina explained, raising her eyebrows.

"Cool! I haven't got any brothers or sisters," Peri said. "I always thought it'd be great to have a little sister."

Poppy sneered.

"Let's unpack, then, shall we, Nina?" Peri continued, flying off the bed and heading towards her own pile of boxes and bags.

Nina and Peri were soon surrounded
by heaps of tutus and tissue paper. They
unwrapped their new ballet clothes,
unpacked their suitcases and giggled
away as if they'd known each other for
ages.

Poppy felt rather left out and very
irritated. She twirled her wand behind her
back and muttered secretly. Suddenly
Nina's and Peri's ballet bags whizzed out
of the room and down the corridor.
Shoes and leotards cartwheeled
chaotically after them.

"POPPY!" Nina shrieked as she
jumped up to grab a passing ballet shoe.
She was about to launch into a lengthy
lecture when Peri burst out laughing.

"Poppy, you're crazy! Make them
come back and do a dance for us!"

Poppy reluctantly found herself
grinning at Peri. She waved her wand
again and the clothes dashed back into
the room, arranged themselves into the

shape of a ballerina – crossover cardigan on top, tutu, tights and shoes beneath – and started whirling round the room.

Nina was not impressed. But before she could snap at her sister the girls were interrupted by someone clearing their throat.

"Quite a spectacle," said a sarcastic voice.

Nina, Poppy and Peri turned to face the speaker. Leaning against the door frame was the blonde fairy who'd stuck her tongue out at Nina in the Grand Hall. She was made to be a ballerina.

Her shiny, slicked-back hair was twisted into a perfect bun, and her long legs seemed to go on for miles. As for her clothes – they didn't look like anything you could buy at Arabesque's. She was the most glamorous fairy Nina had ever seen – except that her face wore a rather ugly smirk.

"What a nightmare," whispered Poppy.

"Shh!" hissed Nina.

"What's that, pipsqueak?" the older fairy snapped.

"N-nothing. She didn't say anything," Nina stammered, giving her sister a prod. "Can we help you?"

"Ooh! 'Can we help you?'," the fairy mimicked. "I doubt it, darling. You're only a scholarship fairy, after all, aren't you? *I* am Angelica Nightshade – your mentor. And I think you'll find that it is *I* who will be helping *you*."

Chapter Six

Angelica's first job as mentor was to take Peri and Nina to meet their class. Poppy told Nina that she would finish unpacking for her, but secretly she had decided to follow the others at a safe distance. She had a feeling she should keep a close eye on Angelica.

The First-Year fairies' teacher was called Miss Tremula.

"She's just right for you new ones," Angelica said knowingly. "She doesn't move too fast for your tiny twinkletoes to keep up."

Peri raised her eyebrows at Nina and giggled.

"What's so funny, slug?" Angelica snapped. "You'd better watch out. The Academy doesn't like upstarts."

"You can't be that popular then," Nina muttered under her breath. But she didn't feel as brave as she sounded.

Peri and Nina went into a lilac-coloured ballet studio where their class was waiting. Poppy hid behind the door, quietly looking in as Nina and Peri went to sit on the floor with the other fairies. Angelica joined the other mentors at the back of the room.

Angelica had been right about one thing: Miss Tremula was not quick on her feet. She was actually incredibly old. She had a brown, wrinkled raisin of a face and silvery hair that didn't seem to want to stay pinned up on her head. Strands of it were escaping all over the

place. She held a golden wand in her hand which she used as a cane. But while Miss Tremula found walking difficult, old age had taken away none of her grace when it came to flying.

When Miss Tremula darted up into the air, waving her wand and giving out instructions to her new pupils, she looked as youthful and dainty as any young prima ballerina. In her youth, she explained to the class, she had danced for the royal court in front of Queen Camellia's mother, Queen Aster. The

new fairies were a rapt
audience.

"Before we begin, I
should like to introduce
you to Mrs Wisteria," Miss Tremula said,
gesturing to another very old fairy, who
was sitting silently behind a piano in the
far corner of the room.

Mrs Wisteria stood up shakily and
curtseyed to the class. I wonder if her
hands are as wobbly as her legs! Nina
thought to herself. She looks far too
ancient to play the piano!

But as Mrs Wisteria struck up the first
few chords of a waltz she earned a
spontaneous round of applause from the
class.

"Time to begin, class!" Miss Tremula

called out, when the clapping had died down.

They began with some easy exercises to warm up.

"Let's come to the barre first, girls," Miss Tremula warbled. "Tummies in! No bananas in my class, thank you!" Peri and Nina giggled. "That's it – backs straight. Right hand on the barre and left hand holding out our tutus. Lovely. Now, plié."

Miss Wisteria started a slow and graceful piece on the piano. The fairies all wobbled down into various versions of

a plié, and came up again uncertainly –
almost in time to the music. Nina was
pleased to see that she was doing as well
as any of the other fairies. From pliés,
the class moved on to work on first
position.

"Now, fairies, can you show me first
position?" Miss Tremula asked.

The class dutifully stood tall, held
their tutus out to the sides, pressed their
heels together and turned their toes out,
just as Nina had tried to teach Poppy to
do.

"Lovely." Miss Tremula beamed.
"Right, now let's try standing with our
feet parallel." Some of the fairies looked
a bit nervous and shuffled from one foot
to the other, not understanding.

"Who knows what 'parallel' means?"
Miss Tremula asked gently.

Nina shyly put up her hand, trying to
ignore the sniggering from the mentors'
bench at the back.

"Good girl!" Miss Tremula smiled encouragingly. "What's your name?"

"Nina Dewdrop, miss," Nina said quietly. "'Parallel' means standing with your feet pointing straight forward. Like this." Nina gave a perfect demonstration, her head held high.

Angelica started clapping slowly and mockingly.

"That's lovely, Nina," Miss Tremula said as she turned to glare at the mentors. "Now, I'd like to see you all practise first position and then parallel, just like Nina. After three,

one – two – three. First position . . .
parallel. That's it! First position . . .
parallel. Well done!"

The little fairy ballerinas all tried to
concentrate on the exercise. Nina found
it hard not to be distracted by the
whispering coming from the mentors, but
she did her best.

Once Miss Tremula was satisfied that
all the fairies were warmed up, she
divided them up into groups and told
them to make up a dance.

"You can choose a well-known dance
or you can improvise," she said. "Be an
animal, an insect – anything you like.
Have fun – but remember to be
graceful."

Nina and Peri were put into a group
with two other fairies, Hazel Leafbud and
Nyssa Bean. The four of them were soon
in a heated debate about what sort of
dance they should work on, so none of
them noticed the mentors sneering and

pointing at them. Nina was very keen on
being a swan and was busily directing
the others into various swoops and dives
when suddenly there was a loud
WHOOSH, followed by a scream.

Everyone looked up to
where the scream was
coming from and saw
poor Nina, hanging
upside down in
the corner of the
studio. Her little
silvery fairy wings
had changed into
huge white feathery
swan's wings, and it
looked as if she was
stuck.

"What is all this
nonsense?" cried
Miss Tremula
angrily. "You may
think it amusing to

make your dance as authentic as possible,
but I will not have any spells cast during
my class, let me make that perfectly
clear! I thought Madame Dupré had
given you the Academy rules this
morning."

"But . . . but, miss—" Nyssa started.

"No buts, Nyssa Bean. You may be
new fairies, but that does not excuse
breaking the Number One Fairy
Academy Rule:

Magic spells must never *be cast*
In any fairy ballet class.
Remember this or you will be
EXPELLED from the Academy!

Pupils are *never* to use magic to enhance
their performances," Miss Tremula
continued. "It is as true here at the
Academy as at any other ballet school in
fairyland. You will only succeed here
through hard work. As you can see,

where novices are concerned, magic and
ballet do not mix," she added, pointing
to poor Nina.

Miss Tremula sighed heavily. "I will let
you off this time," she said, flying up to
help Nina down, "but if I catch you or
any of your friends breaking the Number
One Rule again, you will have to go and
explain yourself to Madame Dupré."

"Yes, miss," Nina whispered, choking
back tears.

Miss Tremula did not like to see fairies
upset on their first day, and she sensed
her class was feeling subdued after the
telling-off Nina had received. She decided
to ask Mrs Wisteria to play some music
from *Cinderella*, which always went down
well with new fairies.

"Staying in your groups, fairies, I'd
like you to improvise a scene from
Cinderella, please. And let's smile, shall
we?" she added cheerfully.

Nyssa, Hazel and Nina decided to
perform the scene where Cinderella is
given the glass slipper to try on.

"You can be Cinderella, Nina," Hazel
suggested kindly. "You've had a tough
morning."

"Yes," agreed Nyssa. "Peri and I can
be footmen, and Hazel can be the
prince."

The fairies were soon whirling and
twirling and enjoying themselves once
again, lost in the music and the ballet
they were performing. Miss Tremula
moved slowly around the room,
encouraging, correcting and praising the
class as they danced.

Suddenly there was a crash and a
scream from Nina's group.

"Not again!" Miss Tremula gasped.

Nina was on the floor tugging at her
leg, and her friends were bent over her.
They looked very worried indeed.

"Get it off! Get it off!" Nina was

crying. Muffled giggles came from the mentors' bench as the class crowded around Nina to see what had happened this time.

Poor Nina was struggling to get something off her foot. It was a real glass slipper! It was far too small for Nina and it was cutting very painfully into her foot.

"What in the name of fairyland did I TELL you about using magic?" Miss Tremula was beside herself with fury and was about to drag Nina to the headmistress when Poppy appeared from her hiding place behind the door. She waved her wand and commanded the glass slipper to disappear. Then, before Miss Tremula could stop her, Poppy shouted, "Nina, Nina, it was Angelica – I saw her!"

"What are you doing in my class?" Miss Tremula demanded.

"I'm Nina's little sister," Poppy said, sticking her chin in the air defiantly. "And I saw who did this to Nina. It was the same fairy who got her stuck on the ceiling earlier. Nina does not need to use magic to perform. She won the only scholarship to get to this Academy. She's a brilliant ballerina – you'll see!" Poppy directed this last remark at Angelica.

Nina was astonished. It seemed quite

out of character for her little sister to stick
up for her. What she's up to this time?
she wondered.

Miss Tremula was also rather
surprised. "Is this true, Angelica? Did you
cast this spell?"

Angelica did her best to look shocked,
hurt and innocent all at the same time.

"Me, Miss Tremula? I don't even
know a spell for glass slippers . . ." She
even looked as if she might cry.

"All right, that's
enough. I think we've
all had
too much
excitement for
one morning,"
Miss Tremula
snapped. "You'd
better make sure there
are no more mishaps
like this while you
are around,

Angelica Nightshade, or it will be you,
not Nina, in Madame Dupré's
office."

Angelica sniffed and nodded, looking
sideways at Nina as she did so.

After class, Nina, Peri and Poppy hurried
to the Refectory for lunch, where they
met up with Mrs Dewdrop again. In
between huge mouthfuls of iced cranberry
buns and gulps of dandelion-and-burdock
juice, Peri congratulated Poppy on her
heroism.

"You were great, Poppy – dashing to
the rescue like that." She slapped Poppy
enthusiastically on the back and winked
at Nina.

Poppy coughed as a lump of pumpkin
bread got caught in her throat. "Thanks
– ahem! Thanks, Peri. You'll have to
watch out for that Angelica, Nina. I
don't think her name has much to do
with her nature, somehow."

"You could be right, there," Peri
agreed. "Is your foot OK now, Nina?"

Nina nodded and smiled. "Peri's right,
Poppy. You *were* great in there. Thanks
for saving me, sis," she said.

Mrs Dewdrop looked anxiously at her
daughters.

"What's been going on? You haven't
been up to mischief, Poppy, have you?"

she asked. "You were supposed to help Nina settle in and find some new friends, not cause trouble."

"Don't worry, Mum," said Nina, putting one arm around Peri. "I feel very settled already. And I've certainly made a new friend. In fact," she added, laughing and flinging her other arm around her little sister, "I think I've made TWO new friends!"

"Yeah!" Peri agreed, smiling at Nina and Poppy. "So have I!"

Now read

Nina Dewdrop has her heart set on a pretty pair of fairy-ballet shoes with daisy-chain laces. Now her mum has promised to buy them - if Nina passes her ballet exam with flying colours.

Then someone casts a spell on Nina's leg and she can't even practise! But her fairy-friend Peri is determined to uncover the culprit in time for the exam . . .

The second funny and magical adventure about Nina and her fairy-ballerina friends!!

Log on to

Nina
Fairy Ballerina
.com

for magical games,
activities and fun!

Experience the magical world of
Nina and her friends at the Royal
Academy of Fairy Ballet. There are
games to play, fun activities to
make or do, plus you can learn more
about the Nina Fairy Ballerina books!

Log on to www.ninafairyballerina.com now!

Collect three tokens and get this gorgeous Nina Fairy Ballerina ballet bag!

There's a token at the back of each Nina Fairy Ballerina book - collect three tokens, and you can get your very own, totally FREE Nina Fairy Ballerina ballet bag.

Send your three tokens, along with your name, address and parent/guardian's signature
(you must get your parent/guardian's permission to take part in this offer)
to: Nina Fairy Ballerina Ballet Bag Offer, Marketing Department, Macmillan Children's Books, 20 New Wharf Road, London N1 9RR

Nina Fairy Ballerina Bag Offer

1 Token

Collect 3 tokens and get your free ballet bag!
Valid until 31/12/06

Other titles available from
Macmillan Children's Books

The prices shown below are correct at the time of going
to press. However, Macmillan Publishers reserves the right to
show new retail prices on covers, which may differ from those
previously advertised.

Anna Wilson

NINA FAIRY BALLERINA

| Daisy Shoes | ISBN-13: 978-0-330-43986-2 | £3.99 |
| | ISBN-10: 0-330-43986-3 | |

Poppy Shire

MAGIC PONY CAROUSEL

| Sparkle | ISBN-13: 978-0-330-44041-7 | £3.99 |
| | ISBN-10: 0-330-44041-1 | |

All Pan Macmillan titles can be ordered from our website,
www.panmacmillan.com, or from your local bookshop and are
also available by post from:

Bookpost, PO Box 29, Douglas, Isle of Man IM99 1BQ
Credit cards accepted. For details:
Telephone: 01624 677237
Fax: 01624 670923
Email: bookshop@enterprise.net
www.bookpost.co.uk

Free postage and packing in the United Kingdom